S0-BYT-716

LET IT GO

LEARNING THE LESSON OF FORGIVENESS

Na'ima B Robert   Mufti Menk

ILLUSTRATOR **SAMANTHA CHAFFEY**

Life isn't always easy
Even when you're small.
You may feel angry, or hurt, or sad
We're only human, after all.

But if you can be just like a tree,
Firmly rooted in your faith,
And always turn to the Almighty
With every trial you face.

You will go through life with a hopeful heart
Aware of all you do.
To be forgiving, patient, sincere and kind
That's my du'a for you.

Mufti Menk

4

It's morning!

So many wonderful things to do,
So many wonderful things to see.
When I wake up, I fill my cup,

A new day is waiting for me!

Soon it's time for breakfast
The meal I love the most.
But my sister gets there before me
And eats the last piece of toast!

How do you feel when things don't go your way?

Allow 'I'm sorry' to make it better. And let it go.

But I don't want to let go.
I want to hold on.
My heart feels heavy
As the day goes on.

At school my friends are busy
Making up a brand new game.
But there isn't any space for me
They don't even call my name.

How do you feel when you get left out?

Allow 'I didn't know' to make it better. And let it go.

But I don't want to let go.
I want to hold on.
My heart gets heavier
As the day goes on.

9

After school, my neighbour comes over
We play football out on the lawn.
But he kicks it too far, here comes a car
And **POP**, my ball is gone!

How do you feel when someone makes a mistake
and you lose something you really like?

Allow 'I didn't mean it' to make it better. And let it go.

But I don't want to let go.
I want to hold on.
My heart gets heavier
As the day goes on.

At supper, I'm telling the story
Of the terrible day I've had.
But all my big brother does is laugh
Which makes me feel so bad.

How do you feel when someone makes fun of you?

Allow 'Will you forgive me?' to make it better. And let it go.

But I don't want to let go.
I want to hold on.
My heart feels even heavier
As time goes on.

13

At bedtime, I pick on my sister
And then she starts to cry.
I didn't really mean to hurt her
I'm upset and I don't know why.

I'm sorry...   I didn't mean it...

I didn't know...   Will you forgive me?

Lights out and I start to think
The day's events run through my mind.
I search for a reason, a wisdom,
And this is what I find:

Not everyone is nice and kind
And makes us feel good always.
But there's one thing I know for sure
We can *all* make mistakes some days.

And forgiving is not a weakness.
It takes a strong person to let go.
I feel my heart getting lighter
As I consider what I now know:

Forgiving is like taking off a heavy bag
that I've been carrying all day long.

And so, I let go.
Astaghfirullah.

Tomorrow is a new day.
Alhamdulillah.

19

Always sleep with a clean heart.
Erase the bad that happened in the day.
Forgive those who have hurt you.
Repent and remember Him always.

Goodnight,
little one!

21

22

Some verses and hadith about forgiveness for you to think about...

**"And seek forgiveness of Allah. Indeed,
Allah is ever Forgiving and Merciful."** (Surah 4:106)

**"And ask forgiveness of your Lord and then repent to Him.
Indeed, my Lord is Merciful and Affectionate."** (Surah 11:90)

The Messenger of Allah ﷺ said, "Allah Almighty said: O son of Adam, if you call upon Me and place your hope in Me, I will forgive you without hesitation. O son of Adam, if you have sins piling up to the clouds and then ask for My forgiveness, I will forgive you without hesitation. O son of Adam, if you come to Me with enough sins to fill the earth and then you meet Me without associating anything with Me, I will come to you with enough forgiveness to fill the earth."

Al-Tirmidhi

Let's talk about the feelings in this story:

sad

disappointed

frustrated

lonely

resentful

angry

25

Write down the things that make you feel angry, hurt or sad. Don't forget to write down the things you are grateful for, that make you feel happy and safe.

Start each day with new hope and a thankful heart.
The Almighty has blessed us with so much!

(Mufti Menk)